Library of Congress Cataloging-in-Publication Data
Pace, Anne Marie.
Vampirina ballerina / Anne Marie Pace ; illustrated by LeUyen Pham.—1st ed.   p. cm.
Summary: Advice for young vampires who aspire to become ballet dancers.
ISBN 978-1-4231-5753-3
[1. Ballet dancing—Fiction. 2. Vampires—Fiction.] I. Pham, LeUyen, ill. II. Title.
PZ7.P113Vam 2012   [E]—dc23   2011026660

Designed by Michelle Gengaro-Kokmen   •   This book is set in 21-point Rolando Opti   •   Art is created using watercolor and pen-and-ink on Strathmore paper
Reinforced binding   •   Visit www.DisneyBooks.com

VAMPIRINA BALLERINA

WRITTEN BY Anne Marie Pace

PICTURES BY LeUyen Pham

DISNEY • HYPERION

Los Angeles   New York

If you are going to be a ballerina,
  you have to do more than wear a tutu
  and dream about dancing.

Your first step is
finding the right ballet school.

I'd suggest . . .

an evening class.

If you're worried about meeting the other dancers,
bring along a friendly face or two—

but leave your pets at home.

They can be distracting.

And distractions
make Madame
very cross.

If you still have
cold feet,

don't be dismayed.

Dancing will warm them right up.

Once class begins, keep your eyes and ears open

and your mouth closed.

The sight of your fangs

might make the other dancers forget fifth position.

POOF!!!

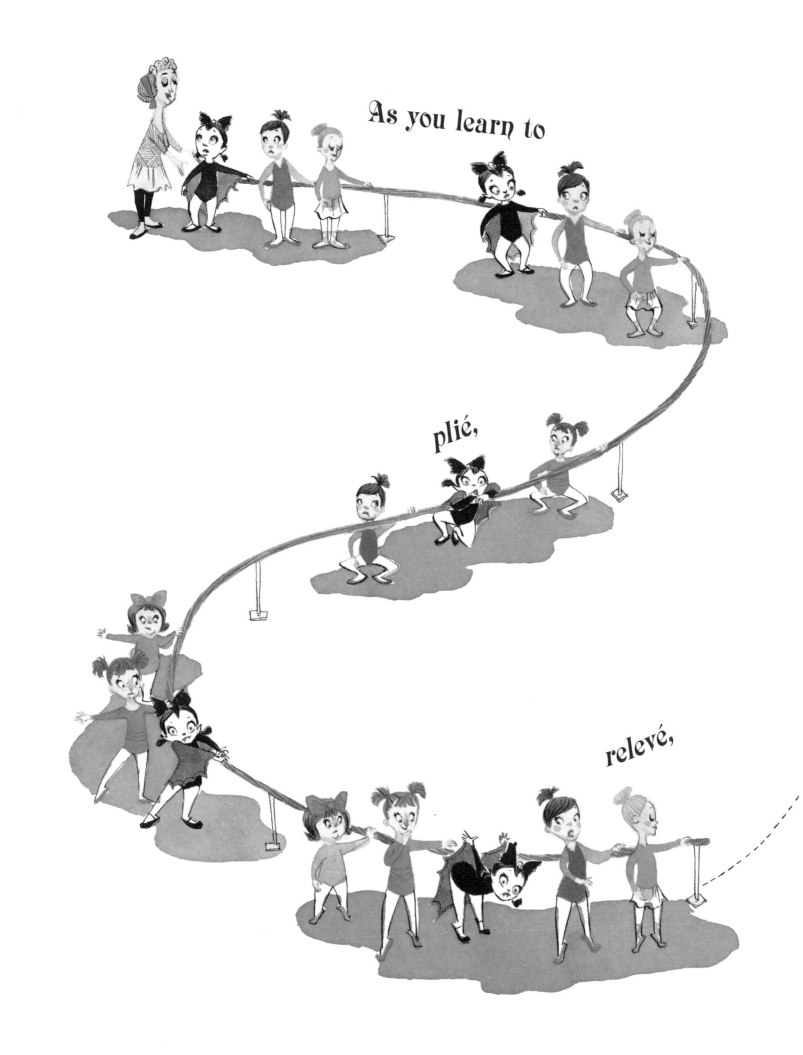

As you learn to

plié,

relevé,

and

arabesque,

be careful not to overshadow
the other dancers.

Like you, everyone will be
trying her best.

And a mistake
here

or there . . .

POOF!!!

is not a reflection on your talent.

Just follow Madame's instructions,
and by the end of class,
your pirouettes
will be practically perfect.

Before you leave,
pay respect to Madame.
A curtsy is customary.

But be careful!

Don't trip
on your cape.

As Madame says,

Whatever happens,
don't be discouraged.
The road to ballerinadom
can be bumpy,

but it doesn't
matter if you take
one giant leap

or many tiny steps,

Plié, relevé...

as long as you are moving toward your goal.

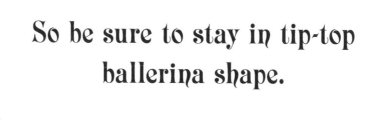

So be sure to stay in tip-top ballerina shape.

Always drink plenty of water and eat healthy meals.

Always get a good day's sleep.

And, as Madame says,
always move with your head held high.

But most important of all:

Practice!

Practice!

PRACTICE!

Before you know it,
it will be time for your debut.

You'll need a costume for the Big Night.

And when you arrive
backstage,

you may get a touch of stage fright.

Remember that the audience . . .

will be just as nervous as you are—
until the lights dim . . .

resist the temptation

And even though it
would make your
grand jeté most impressive,

the music swells,

and the curtain opens.

Even without wings, you can leap higher than you think.

to turn into a bat.

At the end of the dance,
the music will fade.
The audience will applaud
and shout, "Brava!"

Take a well-earned bow,
for you will have become
that rarest of creatures—

A BALLERINA.